THE LITTLE REGENERATIVE FARMER

BY
LAUREN LOVEJOY

© Copyright 2022 by Lauren Lovejoy- All rights reserved.

Without the prior written permission of the Publisher, no part of this publication may be stored in a retrieval system, replicated, or transferred in any form or medium, digital, scanning, recording, printing, mechanical, or otherwise, except as permitted under 1976 United States Copyright Act, section 107 or 108. Permission concerns should be directed to the publisher's permission department.

Legal Notice

This book is copyright protected. It is only to be used for personal purposes. Without the author's or publisher's permission, you cannot paraphrase, quote, copy, distribute, sell, or change any part of the information in this book.

Disclaimer Notice

This book is written and published independently. Please keep in mind that the material in this publication is solely for educational and entertaining purposes. All efforts have provided authentic, up-to-date, trustworthy, and comprehensive information. There are no express or implied assurances. The purpose of this book's material is to assist readers in having a better understanding of the subject matter. The activities, information, and exercises are provided solely for self-help information. This book is not intended to replace expert psychologists, legal, financial, or other guidance. If you require counseling, please get in touch with a qualified professional.

By reading this text, the reader accepts that the author will not be held liable for any damages, indirectly or directly, experienced due to the use of the information included herein, particularly, but not limited to, omissions, errors, or inaccuracies. As a reader, you are accountable for your decisions, actions, and consequences.

Once there was a little girl named Lina. Lina was your average little girl, she loved animals, playing outside, and her friends and family.

One day her mom and dad took her to a farm near their home. Lina loved the animals.

"Mom, Dad, I want to have a farm!"
she said.
"Oh Lina, that's wonderful but farms
are a lot of work!"
her Mom said.

They left the farm and went home.
Lina thought and thought about what her parents said.
At dinner, she repeated "Mom, Dad, I really want a farm."
They smiled to each other and reassured her it was a lot of work and the subject again passed.

The next morning,
Lina had found a book in her collection about chickens
and brought it to her parents. Same request,
"Mom, Dad, I want to have a farm with chickens!"

After a few weeks, her mom and dad finally caved
and bought her a few chickens and a little coop. Lina was overjoyed.
Every day she would make sure the chickens had fresh water and food.
She talked to them, told them about her day
and made sure they had everything they needed.

A few weeks later,
Lina came running up to her mom and dad with a book.
"Mom Dad, this farmer says
you are supposed to move your chickens."
"What do you mean move the chickens?" they asked.

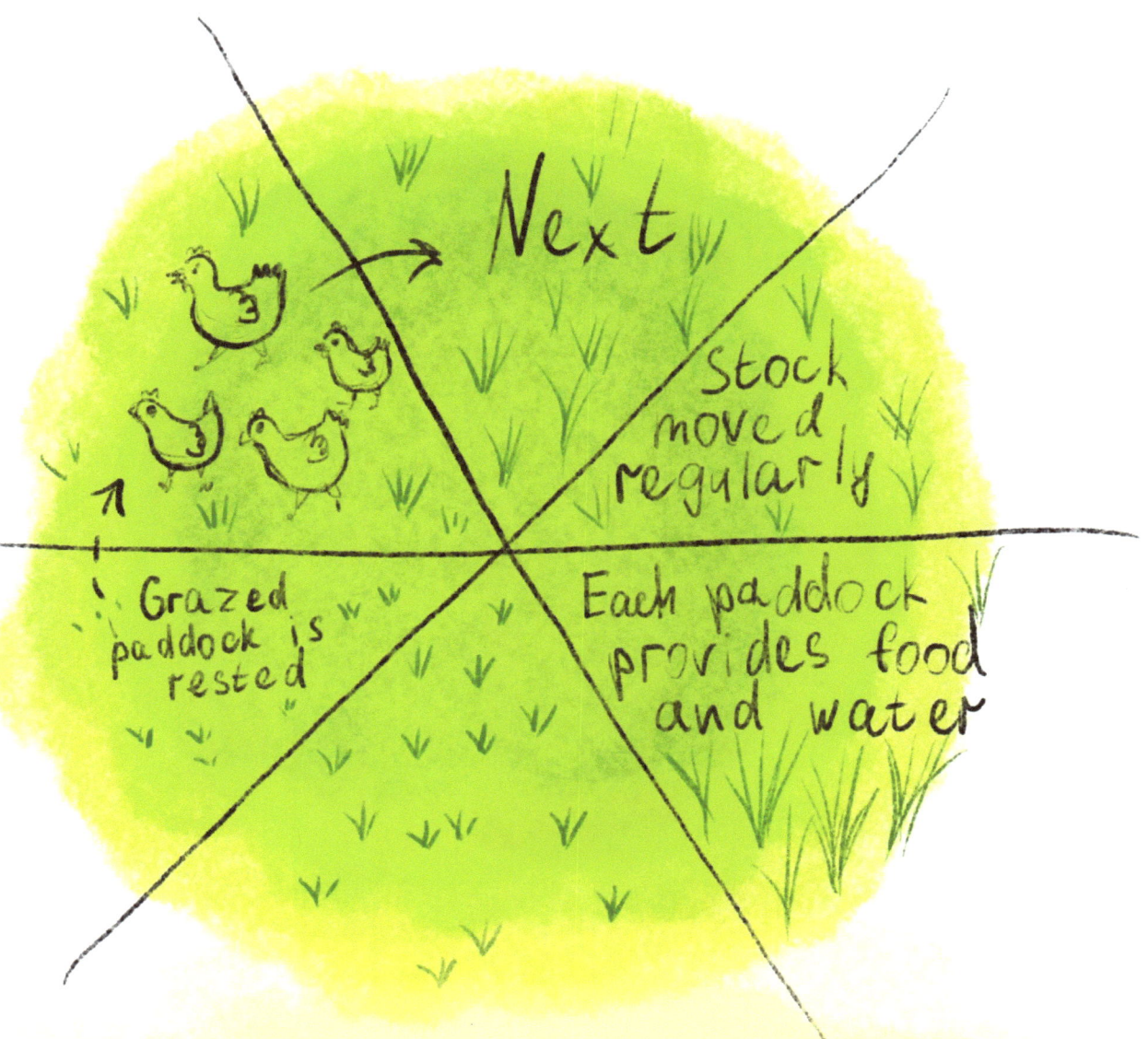

"It says they need fresh grass."
"Well sweetie, I don't think they really do." They responded.
"But I want them to be happier." she said.

After a few weeks, Lina's persistence paid off and, with her parents help, put some wheels on her chicken coop.
Every day she moved the coop to a new patch of grass for the chickens to eat.

Her parents were happy to see that through their daughters' efforts they were spending less money on chicken food and the eggs tasted better, but the grass was growing and growing and the neighbors began to talk and complain.

One day, they sat Lina down to talk to her about how they needed to cut the grass because the neighbors didn't like it.
"Did you tell them that its for my chickens?" she asked.
"Yes, but they like short grass." they said.
"Why?" Lina asked.
"I'm not sure but that's just the way things are," her parents said.

Lina sat frustrated as the next day her parents mowed down a large part of the yard. She couldn't understand why it bothered other people.

She thought about it all night and the next morning she popped up early and headed for the chicken coop.

She grabbed some eggs from her chickens and headed over to her neighbor's house, walked briskly up to their front door and knocked.

As they came to the door she said "Excuse me, I'm sorry to bother you but my Mom and Dad said my grass was bothering you and I wanted to give you some eggs. My chickens make them and they are delicious."

The neighbors accepted and thanked her for sharing her eggs with them.

Lina proudly trotted them back to her home and backyard and told them all about her chickens and how she moved them everyday and how much they liked it and how it made the grass grow tall.

The neighbors were impressed with this little girl's initiative and apologized to her parents that they had complained. They even offered to buy some of Lina's eggs once a week! Lina was delighted.

Next spring, Lina was excited to start planting a little garden. In a spot where the chickens had been eating, Lina took little seeds and placed them gently in the ground. Everyday she waited and soon little spouts appeared.

As time went on, Lina grew more and more things. She planted trees to shade her chickens. She learned to plant flowers beside plants to keep away pests. With her chickens help and care, her garden began to thrive!

Soon was sharing her food with the whole neighborhood.

One day a surprise big storm came. The winds howled and the rain came down in sheets all through the day and into the night. The next day when she woke up all of her plants were fallen over and soaked from the storm.

She sat on the stoop with her chicken, dismayed at all her hard work undone. Her parents watched, disheartened for their daughter.

As Lina, frustrated, got up off the step and started to work on her garden again. Her parents snuck off to the neighbors to let them know what had happened.

Within an hour, all the neighbors came to Lina's house to help her rebuild her garden.
Lina was delighted at all the help and with a few hours of everyone's help, what could be salvaged had been and new seeds had been planted.

In the next few weeks, her garden grew back even stronger and with more food than before! She went door to door sharing the abundance of food with all her neighbors.

At the end of one of these trips, she sat on the stoop looking out over her garden and chickens. Her mom and dad came to sit down beside her.

"You had a pretty big day Lina, did you enjoy it?" they asked.
"I did very much." She said.
"Well you got your garden back, your chickens are happy. What are you going to do next?" they asked.

**To support farmers like Lina,
visit Regenerative Farmers of America
to support a regenerative farm near you.**

www.RegenerativeFarmersofAmerica.com

Want to try some regenerative activities at home?

Visit our website for a free list of children's activities.

From bugs & bees to biodiversity, check out our activities to get children involved in regenerating!

Visit
RegenerativeFarmersofAmerica.com/edu-activites

Principles of Regenerative Agriculture:

- **Reducing Soil Disturbance:** Minimize tillage and reduce soil disturbance.
- **Covering the Soil:** Crops protect the soil surface from sun rays and frost and prevent rain from washing it away. It will improve the soil's water retention capacity & accelerate the nutrient cycle.
- **Keep Live Roots in the Soil year-round:** Plant roots will produce nutrition for the soil food web as well as many other benefits like water retention, keeping soil from washing away, and more.
- **Diversity:** Farming a diverse range of crops, animals, & organisms can ensure a balance of soil nutrients. Crop rotation, companion cropping, and cover cropping are a few ways to achieve it.
- **Integrate Livestock:** Animals can help the soil by dispersing seeds and breaking capped soil, and stimulating plant growth.

CPSIA information can be obtained
at www.ICGtesting.com
Printed in the USA
LVHW070443050123
736520LV00006B/12